Sassafrass Jones

& her forever friends

ABC

For Unforgettable Sunshi xo

AUTHORS
Cathleen Smith-Bresciani
&
Rebekah Kaufman

PHOTOGRAPHY
Tomas Espinoza

SET DESIGN
Christopher McClellan

GRAPHIC DESIGN
Michelle Manfre

This book is dedicated to:
MY "FOREVER FRIENDS"
SHELLEY GOLDBERG—WHO GAVE ME THE INSPIRATION FOR THIS BOOK
MY FRIENDS AT STEIFF NORTH AMERICA—WHO OFFERED OVERWHELMING SUPPORT

MY HUSBAND
FOR HIS ENDURING PATIENCE WITH MY
"PROJECTS" FROM THE HEART

This book is in memory of:
ROBIN HORNE
WHO GAVE ME MY FIRST STEIFF ANIMAL

I'm grateful to Team Sassafrass:
CHIP HORNE, KATHARINE CARROLL, SHANA SCALA,
& ALYSON LONGSHORE

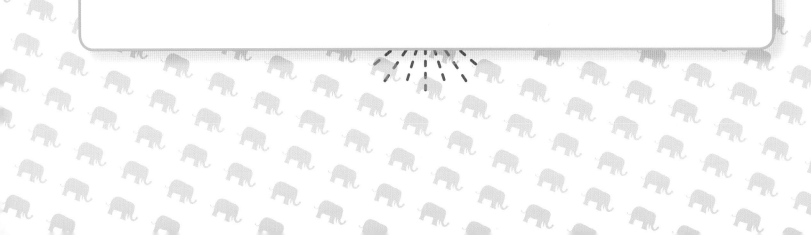

C'mon, let's play… seems to beam from the face of each animal, doll, or bear ever produced by Steiff!

Located in rural southern Germany, and with roots in toy production stemming back as early as 1880, this world-renowned company was founded by seamstress and entrepreneur Margarete Steiff. Steiff's famous button-in-ear playthings have remained favorites ever since 1902, when Steiff invented the jointed Teddy bear that we know and love today.

In addition to being beloved childhood companions, Steiff toys for more than a century have been the stars of countless displays, print advertisements, and children's tales—perhaps in part due to their charming personalities and adorable good looks! It is no surprise that these treasures caught the eye of Cathleen Smith-Bresciani as a little girl, and that they continue to fill both her home and her heart decades later. Cathleen—the creative spirit who brought this book project to life—has playfully noted that, "Steiff treasures simply cannot take a bad picture and unlike most of us need no 'hair and makeup' to look their best on public display."

Steiff's bears debuted in children's literature in 1907, making their first appearance in Sara Tawney Lefferts's *Mr. Cinnamon Bear*. Since then, Steiff animals have taken center stage in many classic stories. Perhaps the most beloved literary Steiff character of all is Steiff's "Jackie" cub, who played the role of the "Little Bear" character from Dare Wright's legendary and award-winning series of children's books from the late 1950s.

So now it's time to take a fresh look at some of Steiff's most endearing and collectible vintage items. Building on a rich legacy of creativity and appeal, Smith-Bresciani gives us an A-to-Z parade, reminding us why Steiff bears and animals still call to collectors of all ages, as well as remain in a class entirely to themselves.

Teddy hugs,
Rebekah Kaufman
Consultant Archivist, Steiff North America

Aa

alligator
al·li·ga·tor
ENGLISH

alligator
alee·gah·tore
FRENCH

caimán
kai·mahn
SPANISH

alligator
ali·gatore
GERMAN

鳄鱼鳄
è yú
CHINESE

ワニ
wani
JAPANESE

Artistic Alligator

~ ALLIGATOR ~

THIS GREEN GOOFY PAINTER HAS SUCH WONDERFUL STYLE...
AND WHO CAN RESIST HIS THOUSAND-TOOTH SMILE?

Steiff's "Gaty" was made in 6 and 12 inches from 1957 through 1974; he also was produced as a hand puppet around the same time. Steiff collectors find his vivid coloring, felt fins and claws, and happy grin totally irresistible!

SASSY STEIFF FACTS

Bb

bear
bear
ENGLISH

ours
oorse
FRENCH

oso
oso
SPANISH

bär
bear
GERMAN

熊
xióng
CHINESE

クマ
kuma
JAPANESE

Bear in Bonnet

~ BEAR ~

**CHECK OUT MY HAT, WITH ITS FRILLS AND FINE LACE—
IT HELPS KEEP THE SUN OFF MY PRETTY BEAR FACE!**

This fuzzy friend is Steiff's "Mr. Cinnamon." This particular version is a modern replica of a Steiff bear originally made in 1903. The original Mr. Cinnamon was used in the book *Mr. Cinnamon Bear* by Sara Tawney Lefferts. This story was published in 1907 and was the first tale to feature Steiff animals.

SASSY STEIFF FACTS

2

Cc

cat
cat
ENGLISH

chat
sha
FRENCH

gato
ga·toe
SPANISH

katze
kat·za
GERMAN

猫
māo
CHINESE

ネコ
neko
JAPANESE

Cats in Couture

~ **CAT** ~

**THIS SWEET SITTING "SUSI" IS ONE LOVELY KITTY;
HER GREEN EYES AND PINK NOSE HELP MAKE HER SO PRETTY!**

Steiff's "Susi" cat was made in five sizes ranging from 4 to 9 inches from 1948 through 1978, and is a classic favorite today among many collectors. Her pattern has its origins in a Steiff cat pattern that debuted in 1936.

SASSY STEIFF FACTS

dog
dog
ENGLISH

hund
hund
GERMAN

chien
she·en
FRENCH

狗
gǒu
CHINESE

perro
pear·row
SPANISH

イヌ
inu
JAPANESE

Dog with Desserts

~ DOG ~

**WHO IS THIS DOG SERVING PIES, CAKES, AND STRUDEL?
SHE GOES BY THE NAME OF SNOBBY THE POODLE.**

Steiff introduced this puppy pattern in gray and black in 1953 in five sizes ranging from 4 to 17 inches. Snobby was such a popular design that she was soon being made as a large ride-on toy, a puppet, and other cozy playthings. She was produced through 1974.

SASSY STEIFF FACTS

Ee

elephant
el·e·phant
ENGLISH

elefant
ee·lee·font
GERMAN

éléphant
el·e·fon
FRENCH

大象
dà xiàng
CHINESE

elefante
el·ef·ahn·tay
SPANISH

ゾウ
zou
JAPANESE

Elephant Embroidering

~ ELEPHANT ~

THIS ELEGANT ELEPHANT CLEARLY HAS SPUNK; CHECK OUT HER PERT EARS AND HER POINTING-UP TRUNK!

Steiff manufactured this beloved and very popular elephant design in five sizes ranging from 3 to 14 inches from 1950 through 1978. Elephants are extremely important to Steiff; as a matter of fact, the very first animal made by the company was an elephant in 1880!

SASSY STEIFF FACTS

Ff

frog
frog
ENGLISH

grenouille
gren·oo·ee
FRENCH

rana
rah·nah
SPANISH

frosch
frosh
GERMAN

青蛙
qīng wā
CHINESE

カエル
kaeru
JAPANESE

Frogs Frolicking on Fauna

~ FROG ~

IT'S EASY BEING GREEN WITH THIS PLAYFUL FROG PAIR;
THEY'RE CHILLIN' ON LILY PADS INSTEAD OF A CHAIR.

Mama on the left is Steiff's 13-inch "Cappy," who was produced from 1979 through 1984. Her crown prince on the right is "Froggy," who was made in 3 and 4 inches from 1953 through 1975. Both are manufactured from a soft, synthetic material called "trevira velvet," a popular toy-making fabric at Steiff in the 1970s and early 1980s.

SASSY STEIFF FACTS

Gg

giraffe
gi·raffe
ENGLISH

girafe
gee·raff
FRENCH

jirafe
hee·rah·fah
SPANISH

giraffe
gee·raffa
GERMAN

长颈鹿
cháng jǐ lù
CHINESE

キリン
kirin
JAPANESE

Glamorous Giraffes

~ GIRAFFE ~

THESE TALL, PRETTY LADIES LOVE CLOTHES WITH A PASSION; THEY'RE THE PERFECT ZOO SISTERS TO MODEL HIGH FASHION!

These Steiff giraffes were made in five sizes ranging from 6 to 30 inches from 1953 through 1974. The smallest size was made from velvet while the larger versions were made from mohair, a woolen fabric. Steiff also is famous for their life-like and life-sized giraffes, some of which stand more than a whopping 8 feet tall!

SASSY STEIFF FACTS

7

Hh

hippopotamus
hip·po·pot·a·mus
ENGLISH

hippopotame
ee·po·po·tum
FRENCH

hipopótamo
ee·po·po·ta·mow
SPANISH

Hollywood Hippo

nilpferd
nea·fard
GERMAN

河马
hé mǎ
CHINESE

カバ
kaba
JAPANESE

~ HIPPOPOTAMUS ~

I'M A CELEBRITY FOR SURE, AND YOU MUST KNOW MY NAME... I EVEN HAVE A STAR ON THAT BIG "WALK OF FAME"!

Steiff's "Mockie" hippopotamus was made in 6 and 8 inches from 1975 through 1978. Although Steiff started producing and selling toys in the late 1800s, it wasn't until the early 1950s that a hippopotamus finally appeared in the line!

SASSY STEIFF FACTS

Ii

indian panda
in·di·an pan·da
ENGLISH

indischer panda
in·disch·er·pon·da
GERMAN

panda indien
ponda·an·dee·en
FRENCH

印度熊猫
yìn du xióng māo
CHINESE

panda indio
panda·india
SPANISH

インドのパンダ
indo no panda
JAPANESE

Indian Panda Iceskating

~ INDIAN PANDA ~

NOT EVERY PANDA IS JUST BLACK AND WHITE;
MY GOLD HAT AND RED COAT LIGHT UP THE NIGHT!

This rare Indian Panda on-the-go is Steiff's "Pandy," who was made in 4, 7, and 10 inches from 1963 through 1964. Indian Pandas in real life can be found in a few places in southern and central Asia, and are an endangered species.

SASSY STEIFF FACTS

Jj

jaguar
jag·uar
ENGLISH

jaguar
jag·war
FRENCH

jaguar
hag·uar
SPANISH

jaguar
ya·gua
GERMAN

美洲虎
měi zhōu hǔ
CHINESE

ジャガー
jagā
JAPANESE

Jaguar Playing Jacks

~ JAGUAR ~

**THIS SWIFT SPOTTED JAGUAR IS READY TO PLAY;
HE'S PRACTICED HIS GAME ALL NIGHT AND ALL DAY.**

Steiff produced this cool cat in 4, 6, and 7 inches from 1954 through 1974.
Each one of his realistic spots was painted on by hand!

SASSY STEIFF FACTS

Kk

kangaroo
kan·ga·roo
ENGLISH

känguru
cang·gur·roo
GERMAN

kangourou
kun·goo·roo
FRENCH

袋鼠
dài shǔ
CHINESE

canguro
can·goo·row
SPANISH

カンガルー
kangarū
JAPANESE

Kangaroo Knitting

~ KANGAROO ~

A NEW JOEY'S COMING—A GIRL I THINK!
THAT'S WHY I'M KNITTING AND PURLING IN PINK.

This bouncing beauty is Steiff's "Linda" Kangaroo, who was manufactured in 6, 11, and 20 inches from 1967 through 1974. The two smaller kangaroos had plastic joeys while the biggest version had a velvet joey.

SASSY STEIFF FACTS

Ll

lobster
lob·ster
ENGLISH

homard
oh·mar
FRENCH

langosta
lan·go·sta
SPANISH

hummer
who·ma
GERMAN

龙虾
lóng xiā
CHINESE

ロブスター
robusutā
JAPANESE

Lobsters Lunching

~ LOBSTER ~

**WE MUST RUN FROM THE FISHERMEN AND HIDE THAT WE'RE RED...
OR WE'LL END UP AS SOMEBODY'S DINNER INSTEAD!**

Steiff's "Crabby" Lobster was produced from 1963 through 1966 in 4, 7, and 11 inches. The smaller versions were made from felt, while the largest Crabby was made from mohair fabric. All had legs that were made from pipe cleaners.

SASSY STEIFF FACTS

12

Mm

mouse
mouse
ENGLISH

maus
mous
GERMAN

souris
sue·ree
FRENCH

老鼠
lǎo shǔ
CHINESE

ratón
ra·ton
SPANISH

ネズミ
nezumi
JAPANESE

Mice Getting Married

~ MOUSE ~

A TOAST TO THE COUPLE, IF YOU PLEASE;
PERHAPS THEIR WEDDING CAKE'S MADE OUT OF CHEESE?

The one mouse that most Steiff collectors want in their house is the company's beloved "Pieps," who was produced in white and gray in 3 inches from 1958 through 1978. The toy store FAO Schwarz produced a series of adorably attired Pieps mice—in outfits including a bridal party, ballerina, princess, clown, Hawaiian dancer, Little Red Riding Hood, and a Miss America Mouse—from 1962 through 1973.

SASSY STEIFF FACTS

13

Nn

newt
newt
ENGLISH

triton
tree·toe
FRENCH

tritón
tree·ton
SPANISH

wassermolch
wasser·mulch
GERMAN

蠑螈
róng yuán
CHINESE

イモリ
imori
JAPANESE

Newt on the Ninth

~ NEWT ~

**THIS NEWT'S MADE OF VELVET THAT'S BOTH BLACK AND YELLOW;
HIS LONG, CURVY TAIL MAKES UP HALF OF THIS FELLOW!**

This sweet Steiff friend measures almost 9 inches long and was produced for one year only, in 1995.
He was made as a promotional item for Märklin, a Germany-based toy company that specializes in model trains.

SASSY STEIFF FACTS

Oo

okapi
oka·pi
ENGLISH

okapi
oh·ka·pee
FRENCH

okapai
o·cap·ee
SPANISH

okapi
o·ka·pee
GERMAN

霍加狓
huò jiā pī
CHINESE

オカピ
okapi
JAPANESE

Okapi Playing the Organ

~ OKAPI ~

**THIS RARE OKAPI IS INDEED HALF AND HALF...
HER BOTTOM IS ZEBRA, HER TOP IS GIRAFFE.**

This rainforest friend appeared in 6, 11, and 17 inches from 1958 through 1970. She comes to life through airbrushing and stenciling—two painting techniques perfected by Steiff over the past century.

SASSY STEIFF FACTS

15

Pp

penguin
pen·guin
ENGLISH

pinguin
pin·guin
GERMAN

manchot
mun·show
FRENCH

企鹅
qì'é
CHINESE

pinguino
pen·gui·no
SPANISH

ペンギン
pengin
JAPANESE

Penguins Parading

~ PENGUIN ~

**IT'S OK TO SEE THINGS IN JUST BLACK AND WHITE,
BUT ONLY WITH LOTS OF PENGUINS IN SIGHT.**

It is no coincidence that Steiff first introduced these cold-loving seabirds to collectors around the time that Rear Admiral Byrd's South Pole expedition was making world headlines in the late 1920s! Here we have Steiff's "Peggy" Penguins. They debuted in 1952 and were produced in five sizes ranging from 4 to 20 inches through 1975.

SASSY STEIFF FACTS

Qq

queen bee
queen bee
ENGLISH

la reine des abeilles
la wren days ah·bay
FRENCH

la abeja reina
la ah·bay·ha ray·nah
SPANISH

bienenkönigin
bee·nan·ku·ne·gan
GERMAN

女王蜜蜂
nǔ wāng mì fēng
CHINESE

じょうおうバチ
joō bachi
JAPANESE

Queen Bee Quilting

~ QUEEN BEE ~

MY SPIDER SISTER WEAVES WEBS WITH HER THREAD;
I PREFER TO USE MINE FOR QUILTING INSTEAD!

Steiff made these 2-inch felt and pom-pon bees in five colors from 1975 through 1981. Starting in the 1930s, Steiff produced many animals as tiny "woolen miniatures" made from yarn. Although they have not been manufactured since the early 1980s, these petite treats remain collectors' favorites today.

SASSY STEIFF FACTS

Rr

rhinoceros
rhi·noc·er·os
ENGLISH

nashorn
nas·horn
GERMAN

rhinocéros
ree·no·say·row
FRENCH

犀牛
xī niú
CHINESE

rinoceronte
ree·no·say·ron·tay
SPANISH

サイ
sai
JAPANESE

Rockin' Rhino

~ RHINOCEROS ~

**THIS KEYBOARD QUEEN IS KNOWN SIMPLY AS "NOSY."
DESPITE HER GRAY COLOR, HER MOOD IS QUITE ROSY!**

Steiff's "Nosy" the rhinoceros was produced in 4, 6, and 9 inches from 1954 through 1974.
All sizes feature dramatic hand airbrushing, an oversized horn, and playful cartoon-style eyes.

SASSY STEIFF FACTS

18

Ss

snail
snail
ENGLISH

escargot
es·car·go
FRENCH

caracol
ka·rah·cole
SPANISH

schnecke
schneck·a
GERMAN

蜗牛
wō niú
CHINESE

カタツムリ
katatsumuri
JAPANESE

Snails Slithering

~ SNAIL ~

**THESE THREE SNAIL FRIENDS TAKE THINGS QUITE SLOW;
WITH A SHELL AS YOUR HOME, THERE'S NO RUSH TO GO!**

Steiff's rare "Nelly" snail was made in 4 inches from 1961 through 1963 in brown or green. Despite her small scale, she was elegantly constructed from a most unconventional combination of materials including; velvet, man-made leather, rubber, and plastic.

SASSY STEIFF FACTS

Tt

tiger
ti·ger
ENGLISH

tigre
tee·gruh
FRENCH

tigre
tee·gray
SPANISH

tiger
tee·ga
GERMAN

老虎
lǎo hǔ
CHINESE

トラ
tora
JAPANESE

Tigers in Tiaras

~ TIGER ~

IT'S EASY TO LOVE BIG, STRIPED JUNGLE CATS; THIS GRR-EAT TIGER TRIO SURELY PROVES THAT!

Steiff tigers have been favorites with collectors since the company started making them in 1915. The tigers on the left and in the middle are Steiff's tiger cubs, which were produced in 4, 6, and 7 inches from 1954 through 1975. The jointed tiger on the right was made in 3, 4, and 6 inches from 1952 through 1959.

SASSY STEIFF FACTS

Uu

unicorn
uni·corn
ENGLISH

einhorn
eyn·horn
GERMAN

licorne
lee·corn
FRENCH

独角兽
dú jiǎo shòu
CHINESE

unicornio
oo·knee·corn·ee·oh
SPANISH

ユニコーン
yunikōn
JAPANESE

Unicorn Under an Umbrella

～ UNICORN ～

**BELIEVING MAKES THIS UNICORN REAL;
HER FELT HORN AND BLUE EYES JUST INCREASE HER APPEAL!**

This gentle and feminine unicorn was made in 7 and 11 inches from 1983 through 1984.
She is one of the earlier "Collector's Editions" Steiff produced for the United States in the 1980s.

SASSY STEIFF FACTS

Vv

viper
vi·per
ENGLISH

vipère
vee·pear
FRENCH

víbora
vee·vora
SPANISH

Viper Wearing a Veil
&
~ VIPER ~

viper
vee·pa
GERMAN

老虎
dú shé
CHINESE

マムシ
mamushi
JAPANESE

I ONLY DON HEADWEAR...DO YOU WANT TO KNOW WHY?
I CAN'T FIND NICE CLOTHES, AS HARD AS I TRY!

This Steiff snake is one tall drink of water, indeed, measuring almost 4 feet long! She was produced from 2002 through 2003. The biggest—and longest—Steiff snake ever made resides in the company's museum in Germany. At almost 50 feet long and 32 inches in diameter, this giant reptile is a huge slide that connects two floors of the museum's interactive play areas.

SASSY STEIFF FACTS

Ww

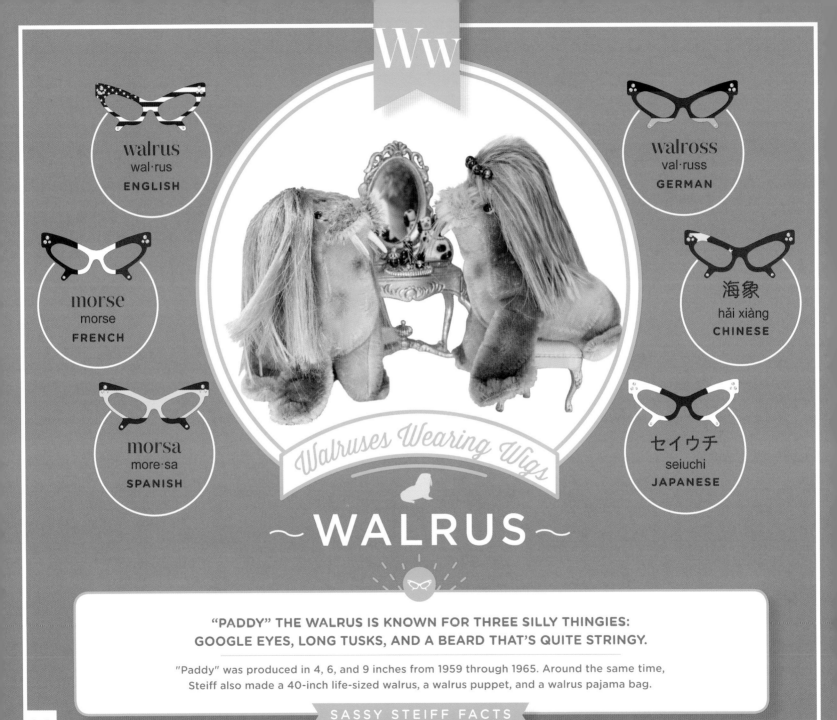

walrus
wal·rus
ENGLISH

walross
val·russ
GERMAN

morse
morse
FRENCH

海象
hǎi xiàng
CHINESE

morsa
more·sa
SPANISH

セイウチ
seiuchi
JAPANESE

Walruses Wearing Wigs

~ WALRUS ~

**"PADDY" THE WALRUS IS KNOWN FOR THREE SILLY THINGIES:
GOOGLE EYES, LONG TUSKS, AND A BEARD THAT'S QUITE STRINGY.**

"Paddy" was produced in 4, 6, and 9 inches from 1959 through 1965. Around the same time,
Steiff also made a 40-inch life-sized walrus, a walrus puppet, and a walrus pajama bag.

SASSY STEIFF FACTS

23

x-ray fish
x·ray·fish
ENGLISH

x-ray-fisch
x·ray·fish
GERMAN

chardonneret d'eau
har·don·nuh·ray·d'oh
FRENCH

X光鱼
x guāng yú
CHINESE

jilguero acuático
heel·gay·ow·aquatic oh
SPANISH

ガラスうお
garasuuo
JAPANESE

X-treme X-ray Fish

~ X-RAY FISH ~

WHEN "X-RAY FISH" IS YOUR NAME, YOUR INSIDES AND OUTSIDES BOTH LOOK THE SAME!

Although Steiff has never made a see-through fish, the company has produced fine finned friends since 1916. The most popular Steiff fish, "Flossy," was made from mohair in red, blue, and yellow in 5, 11, and 26 inches from 1960 through 1981. Three small Flossy fish are pictured here. Steiff also made a soft plush musical version of Flossy—pictured in the upper right—in red or green in 8 inches from 1986 through 1987.

Yy

yak
yak
ENGLISH

yack
yak
FRENCH

yak
yak
SPANISH

Yodeling Yak

yak
yak
GERMAN

牦牛
máo niú
CHINESE

ヤク
yaku
JAPANESE

~ YAK ~

I'VE PRACTICED MY SINGING AND CAN CHANT WITH GREAT CHEER...
'CAUSE THERE'S NOT MUCH ELSE TO DO AROUND HERE!

Size defies with this hearty Steiff soul, who stands proudly at only 5 inches. He was made from 1979 through 1982.
Although most yaks have been domesticated, only Steiff ones can yodel.

25

SASSY STEIFF FACTS

Zz

zebra
ze·bra
ENGLISH

zèbre
zay·bruh
FRENCH

cebra
say·vra
SPANISH

zebra
see·bra
GERMAN

斑马
bān mǎ
CHINESE

シマウマ
shimauma
JAPANESE

Zebras with Zinnias

~ZEBRAS~

**THESE DELIGHTFUL SPRING FLOWERS REALLY PERK UP OUR ROOM...
WITH THEIR SOFT, GENTLE COLORS AND SMELL OF PERFUME!**

Steiff produced these popular zebras in four sizes ranging from 5 to 14 inches from 1951 through 1977. The first zebra produced by Steiff was in 1899; like most Steiff items manufactured before 1903, he was made from fine quality felt.

other PUBLICATIONS

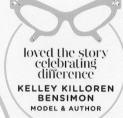

Sassafrass Jones is a total original
ROBERT EVANS
FILM PRODUCER

loved the story celebrating difference
KELLEY KILLOREN BENSIMON
MODEL & AUTHOR

a new childhood classic
PATTI DICKEY
MODERN LUXURY MEDIA

will have your child mesmerized
STORY WRAPS

lovingly detailed photo vignettes
Publishers Weekly

a charming tale of hope
TILLYWIGS

Sassafrass Jones

AND THE SEARCH FOR A FOREVER HOME

Thanks for reading this ABCs book! Please will you give our others a look!
The stars of *Sassafrass Jones and the Search for a Forever Home* can't wait to meet you! They are Mama and Madeline, Steiff "Pieps" mice dressed by the designers at FAO Schwarz from 1962 through 1973, and Sassafrass Jones, a petite pooch made by the world-famous miniature artist Alice Zinn.

SASSY STEIFF FACTS

Cathleen Smith-Bresciani

Rebekah Kaufman

Coauthor and Creator Cathleen Smith-Bresciani happily lives in a home (referred to lovingly as "Animal Eclectic" style-wise) with her husband and four rescue dogs in the Buckhead neighborhood of Atlanta, Georgia. This is her second publication featuring her beloved assembly of Steiff animals and miniatures, which she has been collecting since childhood. A champion of animal charities and four-legged friends, Cathleen continues to raise money for Canine Companions for Independence, The Humane Society of New York, and other local animal charities.

Cathleen had the great fortune to meet Rebekah Kaufman after publishing her first book, *Sassafrass Jones and the Search for a Forever Home*. It was their mutual love for all things Steiff that propelled the collaboration for this ABCs book. Hoping to share the joy that their lifelong Steiff passions have brought to them, they now together look to introduce new generations to the original inventor of the Teddy bear and the legendary company, Steiff.

Meeting the Steiff North America team has been a dream come true for Cathleen. And just as Madeline the Milliner Mouse exclaims in Sassafrass Jones, "...if you stay true to your dream, believe in yourself, and work together as a team, nothing is impossible."

To learn more about Cathleen and her other whimsical Sassafrass products, please see www.sassafrassjones.com.

Sassafrass Jones

Rebekah Kaufman is a third-generation lifelong Steiff enthusiast. Her personal collection of vintage Steiff numbers north of 800.

Rebekah's passion became her vocation when she had the pleasure of working for the U.S. division of Steiff as the Steiff Club Manager. Today, she consults for the company as an archivist, where she leads collectors' events, participates in product development, and authenticates and values vintage treasures. In addition, she is the Steiff expert at James D. Julia, one of North America's top 10 auction houses, where she also runs all administration for the auctioneer's satellite office in Massachusetts.

Rebekah is a regular contributor to several collectors' publications, including the *Steiff Club Magazine*, which is translated into five languages.

Rebekah is the administrator of the vintage Steiff Facebook fan page, the Steiff Worthologist on WorthPoint.com, and the Steiff expert for Auctionata.com and Lofty.com. She is frequently tapped for her Steiff expertise; her engagements have included Theriault's, Christie's of London, Teddy Dorado, *The Boston Globe, The New York Times, Bloomberg*, and the television programs *Inside Edition* and *Pawn Stars*.

Follow Rebekah on her blog, My Steiff Life, at mysteifflife.blogspot.com.
Here you can learn about vintage Steiff finds, Steiff antiquing and travel adventures, international Steiff happenings, and the legacy and history of the Steiff Company.

Rebekah's photo is courtesy of James D. Julia Auctioneers, Fairfield, Maine. www.jamesdjulia.com.

THANK YOU FOR READING

LUXURY KITTEN

44 GRAMERCY PARK NORTH
NEW YORK, NEW YORK 10010

ISBN #978-0-578-15002-4
PRINTED IN U.S.A.